HURRAH FOR ANYTHING

BY KENNETH PATCHEN

HURRAH

Poems & Drawings by
KENNETH PATCHEN

ANYTHING

New Directions

FOR MIRIAM

Contents:

HURRAH FOR ANYTHING

WHERE?

There's a place the man always say
Come in here, child
No cause you should weep
Wolf never catch the rabbit
Golden hair never turn white with grief
Come in here, child
No cause you should moan
Brother never hurt his brother
Nobody here ever wander without a home
There must be some such place somewhere
But I never heard of it

NEVER LIKE THIS
BACK IN MARBLEHEAD

For the bed went to bed
And the chair sat down
Now that was rude, sirs
No way for gents to act
The parlor floor paced back and forth
The wallpaper reached
Out a rosy fist
And almost decabbaged grandma
You kids think that's proper
Oh, oh, here comes a hungry-looking potroast
That blur was just me coming back for my clothes

BRINGING HOME
THE LITTLE BRIDE

Ah! just beyond that next native hut . .
See! there's somebody waving now!
Oh you'll like my family . .
They're an easy ridin' bunch.
One time my old dad just stood
In. one place
Until his suspenders rotted . .
Got himself jailed for disturbing the peace.
Hi there, Buckets! — she's my ma —
Meet Abbybelle . . No, she's *not* got round legs!
This here bit of jazz is called an automobile, stupid!

THE PEACEFUL LIER

I used to flit about hoping
To brush up
On what everybody
Said was so special.
Well, I saw the big shtoonks
Kicking the cans off
The little shtoonks — *and!* . .
Charging them for the service.
Now, I admit that's a pretty special setup,
But if you don't mind I think
I'll just lie this one out in my own way.

DON'T TELL ME

Want to be nice and kind
Don't tell me what happen
I saw a light up in the sky
Never knew they smoked cigars up there
I heard a noise off on the water
Since when the fishes start packin' guns
If you want to be kind and nice
Just don't tell me what's goin' on
I saw the Clean Man a-standin'
'Way up above the world
And what his eyes were wet from wasn't laughin'

WE MEET

We are every so often rustled
By something afar —
In this case, a stretch of watery coast
Along which saunter a Cow
Made of brilliant red roses,
And two heavily bearded schoolchildren;
And in the other, by something quite near —
That is, the imminent presence in us
Of certain vague and shadowy hungers,
Of dreams (and even painful rejoicings),
Which presumably add up to the same thing.

I AM TIMOTHY THE LION

I live in an old sour maple tree
With Happy Jake, who is
A small goldfish;
There is also a short-necked swan,
Two very base players, a bull still wrapped
In pink tissue paper, and a policeman
Shaped like a watering can;
But they're all afraid of sunstroke,
So me and Jake just sit out on our limb here
And shout *Bon Dieu! Bon Dieu!*
Every time the phone rings up in one of those clouds.

TRAVELERS OF NECESSITY

Well you see they spoke Hat and that
Meant if you so much as whispered "kettle"
Clang-bang went everybody's head
With the soup hanging down
Why once a forgetful old man happened
To remark that he'd badly like
To take him a bath
On a ferriswheel
Well now a couple hundred damn near drowned
Before somebody thought to say a common soldier word
Of course, they've had to be on the move ever since

FAR OUT

But he took him down to the roof,
And the other old woman grabbed
Their dripping cigars and glowing tarbooshes
And fed them to the baby.
The Mayor rode by on a large-nosed trout —
It was snowing in his head.
Oh, what is the use of little yellow combs
If your train don't never come?
Oh, you can throw eighty-seven bricks
At any hour your honey ain't around,
It'll still seem as sad and as blank
As an eye that's buried in the ground.

WHAT'S THIS I HEAR
ABOUT CHARLIE?

He'd just come out of his house, see;
Stopped to pull an arrow
Out of his leg . .
You know, since their mama took sick,
The boys put on little shows-like to amuse her,
Bullrun, the Custer bit, maybe a bear-shoot . .
So poor Charlie had just straightened up
When out of the corner of his eye
He sees this big grizzly in the doorway . .
Well, Charlie naturally thought it was one of his brothers —
The fatal power of suggestion, I guess you might call it.

O ! O !

I'm surprise so many eucalyptus tree
Ain't a chestnut.
Be almost more comfortable,
If they wanted to be one,
And nobody minded any.
Like you see so many tired little mule
Can't never be a dragonfly,
And stick his head in the water.
Unless they already are
What somebody else don't want to be,
Or vice versa.

I AM THE CHICKEN

My name is Harry and I like
Everybody; but as a smatter of lack,
There's nobody here, hardly . .
Only some green-cheeked squirrels, whom I fancy
Have lost their boatfares; and a wobbly gaited
Young mouse with a row of sputtering candles
On his back . . Only these, and a little baldheaded man
Who comes every Wednesday with a big shiny bucket
And chases me in and out of the thorny bushes —
Of course he is entitled to his own impression,
But do I have to look like a *cow*
Just because I like everybody!

IT IS THE HOUR

A sigh is little altered
Beside the slow oak;
As the rustling fingers
Of the sun
Stir through the silvery ash
That begins to collect on the forest floor.
It is the hour
When the day seems to die
In our arms;
And we have not done
Much that was beautiful.

WHEN IS A STALKER
NOT A STALKER

Like a downy feather
That floats up the shaft
Of some deserted mattress factory,
Where, during the lunch hour,
A sub-clerk with a weak chin
And a bad cold, phoned his mother
That he would be delayed getting home
Because he had to go see about getting a new radio tube,
And after that maybe stop and examine some clock-pattern
    socks
He'd noticed on sale, I go aimlessly on,
Not really knowing whether I'm running from somebody,
Or somebody's just chasing me because I'm running.

PERHAPS IT IS TIME

Does anyone think it's easy
To be a creature in this world?
To ask for reasons
When all reasons serve only
To make the darkness darker,
And to break the heart?
— Not only of man,
But of all breathing things?
Perhaps, friends, it is time
To take a stand
Against all this senseless hurt.

THE "GREATER GOOD"

Is usually standing near some peaceful tree . .
And may always be found lost
When it comes to "voting"
Or reading the newspapers;
For if he wanted to study up
To be a bloody nut,
He'd choose something more sensible —
Like sticking his head in a buzzsaw.
He's got a hole at either end of him,
Both of which he respects to the point
Of never confusing their functions.
("Governments etc" please copy.)

WHERE TRIBUTE IS DUE

What're you gonna do with people
What kind of eraser
You gonna use on them
Now the mistake's been made
What're you gonna do about it
If you burn them
The stink is bound to linger
Even on those holy-dollar curtains
You've set up to keep them apart
So you're probably right in just letting them die
Like you're doing now

PLAYERS IN LOW SEE

I just had me a talk with Bob Dog . .
He still got his big wobbly tongue hangin' out?
Yep, got him a nice little old lemon ranch now.
He always did want a bald head with hair on it.
You're still not doin' much to me, bub.
I was just thinking . . you know, I —
Sure, I know . .
Look at that damn sneery little sky!
Yeah . .
And all this goddam little — little —
Yeah. Well, be seein' yuh, big shot.

ONLY CHERRIES?

They didn't want me around
Said I couldn't have no cherries
Or watch them pick cherries
Or even stand near the table
Where one of those Kultur-Kookie-Klucks
With the big fat-legged smile
Was fixing to pop a nice red cherry
In on top of his gold spoon
You know I don't like those people
Who act as if a cherry
Was something they'd personally thought up

FLAP*j*aCKS ON THE PIA*zz*A

When Keravvo Jazell invented the "Conductor"
There were still no streetcars or *surging* trains
As we think we know them; instead, each
Householder would twine a bit of old piano wire
Around the bed at night — binding it
Tighter and tighter, until . . *wam! bam!*
The tracks thus made, however, had a tendency
To end in swamps, or up tall trees;
Moreover, many people took to sleeping
With the livestock — on those long winter nights!
In fact, in some more backward localities,
The ticket-seller must often have reckoned
The good Jazell to be not only the father of the baggagecar,
But of a whole new species to ride in it as well.

ALL THE ROARY NIGHT

It's dark out, Jack
The stations out there don't identify themselves
We're in it raw-blind, like burned rats
It's running out
All around us
The footprints of the beast, one nobody has any notion of
The white and vacant eyes
Of something above there
Something that doesn't know we exist
I smell heartbreak up there, Jack
A heartbreak at the center of things —
And in which we don't figure at all

ONE WHO HOPES

Born like a veritable living prince
With small, pink, rectangular feet
And a disposition to hair, I stand
Under the blazing moon and wonder
At the disappearance of all holy things
From this once so promising world;
And it does not much displease me
To be told that at seven tomorrow morning
An Angel of Justice will appear,
And that he will clean up people's messes for them —
Because if he is, and he does, he'll be more apt
To rub their lousy snouts in it.

HOW COME?

You ain't my brother now
I don't trust the way
You stamp your feet on me
I don't shine up
To this devil-goosin' stuff
You been layin' on in my behalf
Oh you ain't my lovin' buddy now
Sometime I think the manner
You come in my house
And dirty-arm me around
Is something I don't particularly cherish

WHO CAN TELL?

Does the resolute little hostler's apprentice
At his mid-morning lunch under a borrowed umbrella —
For who can tell when it may rain, or some overzealous
Pilot maybe drop a camshaft or a couple propeller nuts? —
Of meatloaf and unworked kraut sluiced down
With some overpriced 39-a-quart muscatel . .
Not to forget the wedge of gummy layercake
Which he had traded two excellent kumquats for —
I say, does he ever, in his very inmost self,
Softly murmur: Oh boy! there'll be plenty of snazzy stuff
For every one of us! *an' every man a whole goddam. parade
All by himself!* — Only, I keep forgetting to recall
Just how that's gonna come about . .

A RIDDLE FOR THE 1ST
OF THE MONTH

What has twenty tails and no rear?
What marks time in a haystack,
And yet would beat horseracing hollow?
What distrusts wet rope on principle,
And yet has a burning interest in hanging fire?
What blushes to see two new bikewheels in a rut,
And yet madly yanks at the drawers of old dressers?
What puts a good face on always getting the short end,
And yet saves the real lip-smacking for the fattest?
If you can answer these things, and send me fifty,
We'll both have a lot less to worry about.

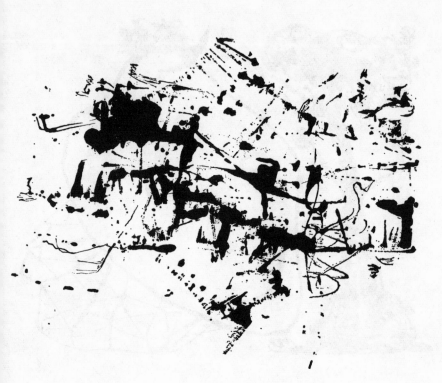

A MORNING IN BIC-BIC..
IN THE GOOD OLD DAYS

Here outside meadow'n moorlet, the goosetooth
Dawn waits by the chipped pink zinc sink;
Waits for Samallyn, who is there, to yearn
Roguishly up the masked trash-treader's funnel:
"Hustle, Mikeleen, you darkish bit of muscled fluff!
The haroohs are again gathering in the nectarish sloobery.
Oh, I tell yuh . . plenty a times I — "
It wercles loosely past the steaming peach-butter vats;
Musses with only scarcely an inaudible clack through
The long gruff shepherd's sister-in-law's youngest daughter's
Sparklingly vague collection of flea circus trapeze miniatures.

NEWS FROM BACK OF YONDER

They ran into the lumber room,
But Tom, whose name was Rodney,
Couldn't make it; so, pushing
Out to the road again, she met
Her mother for the first time,
And an apple blinking to and fro
On a sort of hair, from which
Nothing grew except a tobogganslide.
Wow! soon the lawnchairs will be ripe —
There! feel *those* delicate little ribs!
Ah, nothing quite so pretty as the chest
Of a steaming bowl of tomato soup!

DOGS BOATING

Stroll out the Krinnzer "hoop".
The president of shuffles can wait.
Bind on & brink this woundy mess.
We shoved & shrived them cold plagetts.
At the beginning no kagging was only so.
May it equal if some are out?
Oh no . . Beg under the hands.
There are no stupid births. That's the jat.
Oh that's really drained it, Sally!
And to Then. And to little flutes: (*next*) . .
Him where no turning sifts in soon & jat's no-Jat.

I WENT TO THE CITY

And there I did weep,
Men a-crowin' like asses,
And livin' like sheep.
Oh, can't hold the han' of my love!
Can't hold her little white han'!
Yes, I went to the city,
And there I did bitterly cry,
Men out of touch with the earth,
And with never a glance at the sky.
Oh, can't hold the han' of my love!
Can't hold her pure little han'!

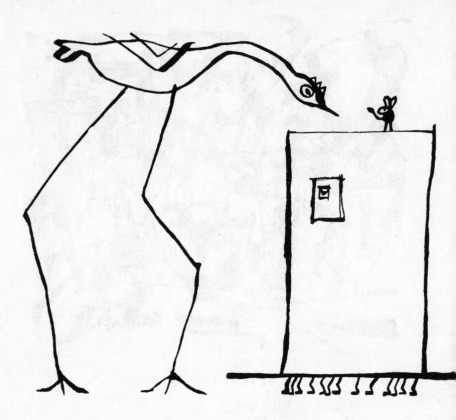

A WORD TO THE SUFFICIENT

Won't do you no good, Mr. Rabbit
Either you pays the rent
Or I perch my fist
On top your carrot-crusher
And quit that chasing through the mezzanine
At all hours
Telling everyone you've got
God's sister coming on a surprise visit
And you need say four or five bucks
For a cab out to the airport
Brother! what a mess you'll be in if she comes on the bus

YES, BLUEBELL, THIS TIME
IT IS GOODBYE

You better scatter
Head for that lonesome window
Ask the pretty lady
Please let us the hell in
'Cause it don't wash off
Poor bluebell's all covered with blood
Her little leaf don't look like a heart no more
Her little leaf look just like something
Some goddam maddog's been crappin' on
You better head out of here but fast

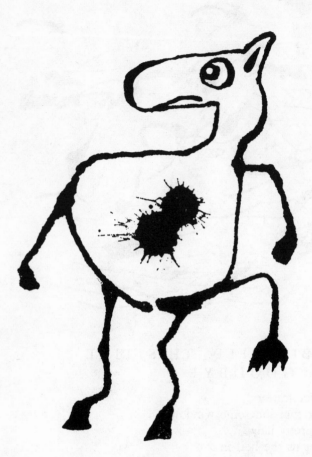

THE COWBOY
WHO WENT TO COLLEGE

There was a cowboy went to college,
Where somebody spilled ink on his horse.
He went to the dean in charge of such things
And was told that that gentleman
Had just popped out to the can again.
"Oh, he has, has he!" cried the cowboy;
"And me thinking it might be an accident —
"Why, hell, it's part of the damn curriculum!"

THE LITTLE MAN
WITH WOODEN HAIR

There was a little man with wooden hair
Who'd sneak into the rear of buses
And holler, "Somebody just ate my mother!"
For that way, of course, he could count on a quick trim
Without having to pay for the broken window.

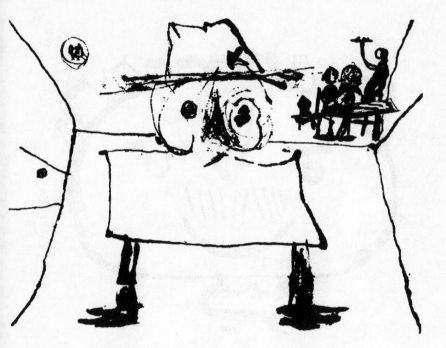

THE MAN-AT-A-TABLE

There was a man-at-a-table
Who had himself a real bang-up time
Getting in and out of restaurants;
Only to have suddenly nervous strangers sit at him,
Often leaving fragments of their abandoned repasts . .
And once even a hurriedly detached hand,
That had been grinding out a cigarette.

THE TAME STREETCAR CONDUCTOR

There was a tame streetcar conductor
Who one day was considerably surprised
To have it suddenly bite his behind;
So next morning he reported for work
Disguised as a broad-minded chambermaid . .
And now lives with the company president's daughter.

THE WILY CARTOGRAPHER

There was a wily cartographer
Driving along with a load of melons
When he happened to notice some old ladies
Playing stickball beside the ruins of a greenhouse;
Rapidly unhitching, and swiftly standing
First on the right leg and then on the left,
He very quickly disappeared from sight.

THE CARELESS LITTLE SPY

There was a careless little spy
Who carried the Secret Code in the same briefcase
With the Master Plan and a wad of dancehall tickets;
Which may explain why some very Big Wheels
Are running about on their rims this morning.

THE FORGETFUL LITTLE
COMMUTER

There was a forgetful little commuter
Who one morning boarded a large sheepish dog
And rode to a splashing stop beside a fireplug;
Arrived home, he hung up his snapbrim wife,
And briefly kissing his hat, said, "Those damn forecasters!
I suppose that cloudburst is their idea of fair weather!"

THE LITTLE MAN WHO
SAW A GRASS

There was a little man who saw a grass
Kicking some beetles off the piano;
So he went to an old sage and demanded:
"Exactly whose chivalry does this defend?"
To which the old sage immediately responded:
"Quick! some water, bub — I smell beard-smoke!"

THE LOYAL STANLEY STEAMERITE

There was a loyal Stanley Steamerite
Who never got invited to parties;
So he let his mustache grow straight out
Until nobody whatever could get past him
Without first deeding over all their property.

THE OLD BRONCHOBUSTER

There was an old bronchobuster
Who read somewhere that the common chicken egg
Was descended from a tiny animal called "the spuze";
This thought so alarmed him that he ripped open
All his old saddles and went around in snowshoes.

THE MAN WHO WAS
SHORTER THAN HIMSELF

There was a man two inches shorter than himself
Who always kept getting stuck in the sidewalk;
And when the curious townsmen came
To yank his arms and crush his hat,
He'd spit in the eye of the lean,
And steal the wallets off the fat.

THE CELERY-FLUTE PLAYER

There was a celery-flute player
Who got himself caught burning fire
On top of some old hoodlum's lake;
They wanted to hit him with a hammer,
But couldn't get up the admission
He would have charged them to see it.

THE GOGGLE-EYED
RABBIT-COUNTER

There was a goggle-eyed rabbit-counter
Who thought to divert himself by pretending to be
The statue-in-nude of the town's stuffiest old maid;
He did this so extremely well in fact
That she is now the father of three little marble generals.

PROMINENT COUPLE BELIEVED
PERMANENTLY STUCK TO PORCH

On impulse, to impress you, and remembering
How much in grade school you liked them,
It was I who had those thousand taffy apples
Delivered to your house —
After so many years!
Me, a humble but honest filing clerk,
And you, O little pig-tailed one, the Mayor's wife!
How was I to know you'd be off vacationing?
Anyhow, think how lucky you are . .
For I might have sent roses —
And then you'd of had big sharp-nosed bees
Lappin' at you instead of them contented bears!

ON THE PARKBENCH

On the parkbench sleeps a small bird-shaped man
In a tophat and orange-purple riding boots flecked
With chocolate, for he had spent the afternoon
In an ice cream saloon. Curled up in his lap
Is a very tall old lady; around them,
On the grass, behind the grass, and smack up
Against the grass, are suitcases, carafes, satchels,
Kegs, tubs, platters, sacks, jars . . and all filled
With the makings of exotic sandwiches. Ah . .
That's why the policeman looks so sallow —
He's a pot of mustard!

ON THE PARKBENCH

On the parkbench sleeps a tiger
With a very tall old lady
In his lap; she is so tall
(And so noisy) that her knees
Have attracted a pair of screechowls
To form on them a nest which sways.
This brings some rabbits, a blazilix,
A camel on a sled, seven frogs, a huge
Red mouse, a policeman, and an even
Taller old lady brandishing an electrified
Trumpet, to the scene; and to us
The timely remembrance of a dinner date.

AND WITH THE SORROWS
OF THIS JOYOUSNESS

O apple into ant and beard
Into barn, clock into cake and dust
Into dog, egg into elephant and fingers
Into fields, geese into gramophones and hills
Into houses, ice into isotopes and jugs
Into jaguars, kings into kindnesses and lanes
Into lattices, moons into meanwhiles and nears
Into nevers, orphans into otherwises and pegs
Into pillows, quarrels into quiets and races
Into rainbows, serpents into shores and thorns
Into thimbles, O unders into utmosts and vines
Into villages, webs into wholenesses and years
Into yieldings . . O zeals of these unspeaking
And forever unsayable zones!

AN "IMPRESSION GAZOOM"

I get a most definite "impression gazoom"
As I comb through my days as an opener
Of Kansas doors and shutter of Wyoming windows;
When you would come bustling out of the shack,
Your eyes like undone cakes grabbing me to pan,
Casting the tanner's abrupt needle into a bush,
Or behind the swing, for Wally Potts, barefoot
As usual, it being a time the brooks ranuvert
Like eager green pinkies along the town's thigh,
To find himself suddenly possessed of half
Laurinda Robert's bra, and standing, perchance,
Quite altogether through the other side
Of that old brick wall, where, was the night fine,
The woodcutters would park their long sleek yellow cars
And war their souped-up radios at one another.

LIKE I TOLD YOU

We headed out to the orchard
And looked a while
It seemed all right
The apples weren't complaining
The Bird of the Mountains
Was strolling around
Making up a little song
Maybe to the sun
Or for his special friends
Or his sweetheart
Or just to himself
And maybe for no reason
That anybody could tell you about
Sort of like I'm doing right now